ALMASI YA KIFO

· · · · · ● · · · ·

LORNA DOWNS AND MAURY K. DOWNS

Almasi Ya Kifo

Published in the United States of America
By Jewel Sky Publications and Productions

Dedicated to

MKD, my husband, my pilot and my soulmate.
You bring out the best in me.
Mahal na mahal kita.
My mother, children and grandchildren,
I dearly love you all.
My sister and brothers, there is never a day that I don't
think of you. I love and miss you kakabagis ko.
— LD

Lorna, Mom, Dad, Ritha, Marcia, Michael, Ryan Kristoffer,
Jasmin, Kristina, Gillian and my dear grandchildren.
You are all part of me.
— MKD

PRAISE FOR ALMASI YA KIFO

"Maury K. Downs triumphantly returns to the literary scene with Almasi Ya Kifo, a riveting follow-up to his captivating debut, The Way You See Me Now. Joining him in the writing of this gripping suspense thriller is author Lorna Downs.

Central to the novel is Paulo Pineda, a seemingly average man navigating the humdrum of life: nursing a crush on his boss, working at a video rental store, and residing with his parents. However, life takes an unexpected detour when a treasure trove of diamonds— the legendary Almasi Ya Kifo diamonds— lands in his possession. These aren't just any diamonds; they carry an aura of mystique. Legend suggests they possess dual capabilities: granting their holder unparalleled good fortune and protection or heralding a cascade of calamities.

For Paulo, the path seems fraught with danger, especially with the diamonds' previous owner, the notorious criminal Joseph Ashe, hot on his heels. Paulo, portrayed as an endearing underdog with an unyielding spirit, consistently finds himself teetering on the edge of peril. Yet, his resilience and sincerity make it impossible for readers not to champion his every move, from evading life-threatening situations to conquering personal insecurities.

The authors' supporting characters, notably Paulo's childhood confidant Tommy Grainger, are painted with equal depth and vibrancy. The dynamics between Ashe and Paulo stand out as they present contrasting facets of humanity.

The pacing is impeccably crafted. Readers are introduced to the ensemble cast, swiftly thrusting them into a whirlwind of high-stakes adventures. There are moments when the tension is palpable, akin to witnessing a vulnerable creature stray into a hazardous zone.

Almasi Ya Kifo is a heart-pounding crime thriller distinguished by its empathetic protagonist. With further installments on the horizon, one eagerly anticipates the ensuing chapters of this thrilling saga. Highly recommended for those seeking a story with depth, intrigue, and heart." — *Literary Titan*

ABOUT THE AUTHOR

Maury K. Downs was born and raised in Los Angeles, California. He has had a rewarding previous career working as a health care provider. His joy is all things aviation, and he is a certificated pilot and flight instructor. He has traveled the world as an airline transport pilot. He holds a type rating in the "Queen of the skies" Boeing 747 and the Airbus 320. When he was a child, he enjoyed telling imaginary stories to his friends and family for their entertainment. He enjoys hearing the humorous cavorts and bold adventures of people's travels. "The Way You See Me Now" was his debut novel, and it is the prelude to this exciting book series.

CHAPTER 1
THE BOSS LADY!

IT'S 5:00 PM ON Friday, September 21, 2001. Paulo Pineda is ending his shift at Megabuster Video in San Bernardino, California. It's payday. He is just completing his last transaction of the day.

"Thank you for coming and have a Megabuster day." He smiles politely as he hands the rental videos over to a customer. Behind Paulo is a sign displaying a less than subtle request. It reads, 'Please Be Kind, Rewind!' They nod and turn to leave.

"Hey Paulo, I have something for you." Karen Loren smiles, approaching Paulo from the aisle of videos behind him.

"The boss lady!" Paulo jests with a smile in return as he turns to look at her, "Coming to bring me something nice, I see." He eagerly receives his paycheck from Karen.

"You're off this weekend, right?" Karen steps closer, "Got plans for the weekend? Doing anything fun?" Paulo looks down towards the floor, avoiding making direct eye contact with her. "Not really." he replies, fidgeting a little from their closeness standing together at the register.

Paulo always feels a little nervous when speaking directly to Karen, because of the affection he has for his boss. He has been attracted to her ever since he started working there three years ago. Paulo hasn't told her how he feels, though he wants to, very much. He's just not sure if she feels the same way about him. He thinks she does, sometimes. Too many mixed signals, he concludes self-consciously. Being his boss doesn't help ease his apprehension, either. If anything, it makes his affection for her seem more inappropriate. Nevertheless, he lacks the confidence to approach her.

"I'm just going to hang out with Tommy, probably." Paulo looks over at his longtime friend since high school, Tommy Grainger, who also works there. Tommy was busy helping someone find a video in the horror section. "We might go see a movie or something." Paulo perks up from his nervousness, sounding a little more assertive. "Maybe we'll go see that Rush Hour sequel. Uh, it's called, uh..."

"Rush Hour 2." Karen giggles.

"Yeah." Paulo nods enthusiastically with a smile. "The first one was really funny."

Karen nodded back. "I saw Jay and Silent Bob Strike Back recently. That was pretty good, I thought."

"Oh yeah," Paulo, smiling more, "I want to see that."

"Well, I hope you and Tommy have a good time." Karen says.

"How about you?" Paulo asks. "What are you doing?"

Suddenly, from a distance Tommy's voice could be heard from one of the aisles of the video store, "What are YOU doing?!" Tommy teases, imitating a popular beer commercial skit. Laughs can be heard following his clever banter from other customers in the store. Paulo shakes his head and chuckles.

"I'm going to visit my best friend in L.A. this weekend." Karen replies, still smiling from Tommy's response. "You guys enjoy yourselves." She turns and walks towards the staff office.

"How ya doin'?" Tommy can be heard engaging young customers near him with his best New Jersey accent impersonation. They respond eagerly in the same character, "How ya doin'?" Their light-hearted improvisation of another television beer commercial brings more laughter in response. Humor is the best medicine in times like these nowadays, considering the nation's current state of affairs.

The horrifying terrorist's attacks occurred only a few weeks ago. The painful and disturbing emotional wounds are patent and eerily surreal for everyone during this dreadful moment in history.

"I'll call you later, dude." Paulo waves at his buddy Tommy. His friend just waves in return. Tommy is busy answering a customer's questions about video games in stock and the newest arrivals to the store. As Paulo walks out the main entrance, he passes a large picture displayed in the front window. The picture shows three firemen tending to the American flag amidst a wall of decimated remains of the iconic World Trade Center, Twin Towers. The caption on the photograph reads, '9-11-01 Never Forget'.

CHAPTER 2
IT'S ONLY MONEY

Paulo had told his mother he was going to work overtime today. But what he really did was cash his paycheck at the bank and head straight to his favorite Native American casino in Cabazon. It was only a short 25-minute drive. He figured he would just stay a few hours. A few hours later however, he's resolved to recovering his $290 deficit.

"Damn!" Paulo rubs his face. "Slots aren't loose today. I'll try the poker machines." As he gets out of the chair an eager elderly woman takes his place.

"Having any luck tonight honey?" The woman smiles. She senses his frustration. "The poker machines are paying, but you can't get a darn seat!" She motions tilting her head towards the area. Paulo makes an attempt to smile humorously in response.

"Good luck." He tells her as he walks away.

Paulo notices the body language of the gamblers sitting nearby at the other slot machines. Nobody's excited. They all look the same, like creatures of addictive habit. All of them, staring expectantly into the mesmeric gambling displays. They constantly feed their wages and hard earnings into the chiming machines, as if they're feeding a cute little animal at a petting zoo.

Just watching the others, Paulo feels that irresistible urge to continue feeding the machines. From his perspective he has to keep at it. Every moment standing around makes him feel like he is missing out on something. Paulo makes his way over to the video poker machines. He's able to find the only seat available and plants himself in it. He feels a sense of relief now that he can get back to business. Cigarette smoke is so thick in the air he can taste it. There is a larger crowd than usual tonight, probably because it's also payday for many others, just like him. Paulo sighs heavily as he inserts his last $35 slot machine ticket into the hungry video poker machine. He's ready for some determined five-card draw gameplay now.

Paulo plays five hands at maximum bet that only yield a mixed pair of 3s at best. He shakes his head, frustrated. After only a couple minutes, his entire paycheck has now been reduced to about half his remaining slot ticket balance. Paulo is feeling more desperate now. His palms are sweaty. He clenches his teeth and presses the deal button again to play a new hand.

The resultant bet dealt causes the video game machine to chime pleasantly, signaling a winning hand. The display is showing 2-3-4-5-6 of hearts. A straight flush! The winning jacks or better hand just paid $125 on his maximum bet. Not bad he thinks. *My luck is getting better.*

Paulo decides to stay just a little bit longer. And the battle of wagers continues. Winnings are up and down. Not enough to get everything back, but just enough to keep trying again, and again. Paulo presses on. He continues his effort to try and recover his losses and restore his paycheck amount. Paulo ends up staying and gambling the entire night to do so.

By 6:15 AM Saturday morning, and after nearly ten hours of gambling non-stop, Paulo decides he has had enough. He looks down at his slot machine ticket. "Two dollars and fifty cents." He mumbles as he stares at the pitiful balance. That is all that remains of his $784 paycheck from the day before. He shrugs his shoulders. "Oh well. It's only money."

Paulo gets up and walks away from the video poker machine, stretching and yawning. Most of the people are gone now, save their collective cigarette smell that heavily remains. Paulo cashes his ticket. He buys a glazed donut and coffee with his meager remains. He shuffles his feet, slowly walking to the parking lot. He finds his car, gets in, and heads for home.

CHAPTER 3
YES DAD

As Paulo walks into the house, he sees his parents sitting at the breakfast table. His parents turn to look at him, then they look at each other, perplexed. The intimate quiet of the morning gets subsequently demolished as Paulo is unhappily greeted by his father, Alejo.

"You're just coming home now?" His father raises his voice slightly at the end of his question. Still holding the utensils over his plate of Filipino fried rice, eggs over easy, longganisa, pandesal, and a full cup of black coffee, Alejo asks, "Where have you been the whole night?"

His father's look demands an immediate answer. However, Paulo doesn't make eye contact. He doesn't even look towards his parents sitting in plain sight. Paulo continues walking, quietly making his way to the kitchen. His parents silently watch as Paulo retrieves a bottle of water from the refrigerator, then turns to walk towards the stairs.

"Don't turn your back on me!" Alejo commands, "I was asking you a question." His voice much louder and his Filipino accent getting heavier now.

"I was at the casino!" Paulo responds with a raised voice as he approaches the stairs that lead to the upstairs bedrooms.

"Don't you raise your voice at me young man!" Alejo responds, glaring at his son, who still has his back turned to his father. At the sound of this demand, Paulo turns around.

"I was at the casino, dad." Paulo is less resolute already, as he respectfully calms his tone. He walks to the table and quietly sits down next to his mom and dad. His mother, Mary gets up and puts some food on a plate for her son.

"Casino?" His father still has a raised tone of voice. He begins to lecture his son, some of which is in his native tongue. "Sos, Marya, Hosep, Paulo (*Jesus, Mary, Joseph, Paulo*)! When are you going to learn?! When are you going to listen?! Kelan ka ba titino, ha (*When will you have sense, huh*) Is this the life you want? Wala ka man lang bang ambisyon sa buhay (*Don't you have any ambition in life*)? You know when I was your age, I already had a good career and was able to pay my own bills and provide for the family."

There's no reply or reaction from Paulo. He is quiet, sitting straight and looking down at the table. The lecture continues.

"Sabi ko na nga ba eh. Dapat sinunod ko ang instincts ko (*This is what I'm talking about. I should have followed my instincts*). To raise you in the Philippines. Ewan ko ba (*I don't know*) why I let your mom and her sister Elvie talk me out of it. Look at you? You can't even pay your bills and still living at home!" His father says, motioning animatedly with his hands at this point.

Paulo's only response is to quietly eat from the plate of delicious smelling food that his mother gently places in front of him. Mary pats her son on the shoulder, smiles and sits down. Alejo gives her a slight glance for the tiny distraction and lack of reprimand assistance. Alejo returns his chastising gaze towards his son.

Paulo doesn't even make eye contact with his wide-eyed, wound-up dad. He simply takes a generous bite of some sweet and tangy longganisa. Just a blink of his eyes is the extent of Paulo's reaction now, besides chewing.

"Walang responsibilidad (*No responsibility*). Walang inatupag kundi casino, video games, casino (*You care about nothing but casino, video games, casino*). You are aging backwards Paulo!" More hand gesturing from his dad.

Mary purposefully interrupts her overly aggravated husband. "Tama na (*Stop already*). So early in the morning, ...abot na sa bubungan ang bp mo (*...and your blood pressure already up to the roof*). Talk later, na lang pag cool na ang head ninyong dalawa (*once you both cool off*)."

Alejo retorts. "Ah bahala kayong mag-ina (*I don't care*). Talk to your son and stop spoiling him. He needs to learn. We are not here forever!" Alejo drinks a mouthful of his now, lukewarm coffee.

Realizing the time, Alejo stands up to leave the table. "We need to talk more this evening, Paulo. Right now, I am going to work." He states. He takes another gulp of coffee. End of lecture, for now.

Paulo raises his head up from his plate. He looks at his father and simply responds, "Yes dad."

Alejo quietly walks out the front door. Paulo finishes the last bites of his breakfast and heads upstairs to his room without making another sound. Mary starts tidying up the dining table and kitchen, quietly humming as she does so. The serenity of the beautiful morning has returned, as if nothing happened to disturb it. Only the sound of Alejo's car driving away is noticeable.

As Paulo swings open the door to his room, he quickly turns and runs back downstairs to find his mother. She's in the kitchen rinsing the dishes before placing them into the dishwasher. She's still humming the same melody.

"Mom!" Paulo excitedly exclaims.

Mary flinches totally startled, "Paulo don't you scare me like that! What is wrong with you? You know I easily get scared. I thought you were going to sleep?"

"Nah can't sleep yet." Paulo replied. Then he asks his mother straight out, "Mom, can I borrow a hundred dollars?"

Mary abruptly stops what she's doing. She shakes the water from her hands and turns to face Paulo, "You asked what Paulo? Have you really lost your mind anak (*son*)? Don't tell me you bet away your whole paycheck again in the casino? Paulo, this is why your dad gets so upset." She says seriously with furrowed eyebrows.

"I know, I know but I will pay you back. I promise." Paulo begs.

"Paulo you always promise. If promises could kill, you would have died a long time ago. You understand?" She says, pointing at him.

"Mom, come on please." Paulo pleads with his eyes, looking at her the precise way he knows will get to her soft side.

"Okay. I will leave it on top of your TV stand. Pero anak (*But son*), this will be the last time I give you money. Your father is right. You need to learn because we are not here to rescue you forever. Anything can happen and whatever that may be, we want you to survive on your own." She replies shaking her head. This is her best attempt at sternly lecturing him.

"Okay mom. I understand." Paulo hugs his dear mother and kisses her cheek. "Thank you, Mom. You are the best!"

"Mmm, I already know that. Go and sleep now."

Paulo prances away like a happy little boy. Mary continues rinsing the dishes. She shakes her head thinking of the way her 24-year-old son is handling his life.

CHAPTER 4
YOU HAVE THE WRONG NUMBER

NOT FAR AWAY in a motel close to the interstate, there is a man contemplating what his next course of action should be. That man is Joseph Ashe, a 50-something, skinny and unshaven fella on the run. He's sitting on the bed looking at a plane ticket to Sao Paulo, Brazil. The flight he is booked on is departing the following evening. Joseph is quiet, emersed in deep thought. Smoke from a lit cigarette in his slightly pursed lips wafts upwards in front of his face. Sights and sounds from the television on the other side of the room catch his attention intermittently. A local news station is displaying repeated images and video from the recent terrorist attacks on the nation. Joseph is not at all interested in the news. His attention is mostly focused on something else, however.

He places his ticket down on the nightstand next to him and picks up a black velvet jewelry box. Joseph opens the case. The same as he has done several times over the past hour just to look, and gloat. He smiles greedily at the sight of its prized contents, flawless diamonds. The gems sparkle brilliantly, irrespective of the poor lighting in the motel room. But these are not your everyday, average wedding ring type diamonds. These diamonds carry a certain, extraordinary mystique about them.

The jewels that are now in Joseph's custody are considered priceless by many experts in the diamond and jewelry trade industry. These diamonds are so rare and the legend such a mystery, that they are tirelessly sought after by many wealthy eccentric types of individuals and gem collectors. They are known and recognized by a very peculiar name. These are the mysterious 'Almasi Ya Kifo' diamonds. Joseph is enamored by their beauty and the high price the rare gems will command and fetch.

The phone in his cheap motel room suddenly rings. Joseph takes a deep drag from his cigarette and exhales. The phone continues to ring. Joseph is in no obvious hurry to answer it. He places his cigarette on top of a metal soap dish, calmly reaches around a 'no smoking' sign on the nightstand and lifts the receiver. There is a slight pause before the conversation begins. A calm voice on the other end tells him to just bring the diamonds back and everything will be okay. Joseph needed no salutation from the caller. He recognizes the voice and immediately knew who it was.

Joseph Ashe has more enemies than he has friends. Truth be told, he is not a popular, likable person. Joseph has a well-documented criminal record going far back, since his early teens and hasn't changed his ways much over the many years. Joseph has become well affiliated with a theft and smuggling ring of shady associates. He and his dubious business partner make decent money, selling stolen and knock-off brand jewelry items at various tradeshows around the country. Now, however, Joseph has decided to part ways and go into business for himself. In a manner of speaking.

He stole the mysterious Almasi Ya Kifo diamonds from his thieving business partner's jewelry store located in Las Vegas, Nevada. His partner had serendipitously come into possession of them very recently. Joseph tried to make it look like the store was robbed and vandalized in the process. His greedy business partner and his crooked associate weren't so easily fooled. And now they are going after him.

There is another moment of silence before Joseph replies. He coughs as he tries to mask his voice. He responds in a made-up accent in a spontaneous attempt to disguise his tone. "Who is this? What? You have the wrong number." He hangs up firmly and pulls the phoneline in the wall out from the phone, laughing. He thinks for a moment then stands up and hurriedly begins to pack some clothes strewn on the bed into a large backpack ready to leave. Joseph's thoughts immediately reflect on someone he'd very recently told about his travel plans.

"Beth!" He says her name aloud. "I just know it's that no good, backstabbing woman. She sold me out! Shit!" Joseph assumes, shaking his head. He just knew it had to be his whiney, on-and-off again, barfly of a girlfriend. "She told them!"

CHAPTER 5
WE JUST GOT PAID, BRO

LATER THAT DAY Paulo is hanging out at Tommy's apartment. Paulo is looking at computer magazines. Tommy is working on a desktop computer he's putting together. They talk about life in general. They talk about their boss, Karen.

Tommy asks, "Does Karen even know how you feel?" He stops working on the open computer case and looks at Paulo. "I mean, it's been a while now. So, when are you going to ask her out and tell her how you feel, man?"

"I dunno man." Paulo scrunches his lips and looks down. "I'm not so sure it's the right time right now."

Tommy shrugs his shoulders, motioning with his hands, "Then, when? When is it ever going to be the right time? I mean, we've all gone out together as a group, as friends and all. But like, it's time for you to go at it alone, I say." He shakes his head, looking at his longtime friend, Paulo.

"I just don't have the confidence like you, Tommy." Paulo replies, shaking his head. He genuinely looks up to his buddy. He considers Tommy a real woman charmer, much more than himself. Paulo lacks the confidence. "I just don't think I'm there, man. Not quite there, yet."

"Yeah?" Tommy says self-confidently, "Well, I would have been her boyfriend for sure by now, if I were you."

Truth is Tommy hasn't had a girlfriend for almost four years now. Not since he was dumped by his long-time nerdy high school sweetheart. Both these young men always talk this way when it comes to romance. Neither of them has ever experienced true love. They still carry on like little boys, instead of twenty-something year old men. Which still isn't saying much. Nevertheless, life still has a lot to teach them, especially when it comes to being in love with a sincere, loving woman.

"My man," Tommy continues to boast, providing his wealth of lack of experience, "you need to learn. Women want to be talked to and they all want a boyfriend. Women need attention. They need a man." Tommy nods in approval of his own advice.

"Yeah, I hear you, man." Paulo replies, "I dunno. I just get so…" He shrugs his shoulders, "I get nervous when she's around. It's like I can't think or something."

Tommy chuckles and shakes his head. Then, Paulo's new Ericsson T66 mobile phone he got from his mom starts to ring. Paulo takes a call from a friend regarding a multilevel wagering gimmick he is participating in and how it is doing.

"Hey, Jacqueline, uh huh…" Paulo is listening intently. She tells him the progress of the game and his 'investment.' Paulo really enjoys these types of games that take advantage of those joining later who make a wager further along after other participants. "Very nice." He grins with glee. "Yes, roll it over, I'm staying in. Okay, sounds good. Talk later." The call ends quickly, and Paulo turns his attention to his friend, Tommy. "I'm stoked."

"Who was that?" Tommy is back to working on his computer.

"My friend. She's a nurse that works with my mom at the hospital. She was just updating me on a game I'm playing."

"She works at Pleasant Hills Hospital?" Tommy asks, still concentrating on what he's doing. "With your mom? What game?"

"It's that airline game I told you about. I've moved up to first class now. You wanna play? There's still time, but you better hurry." Paulo says, sounding a bit insistent.

Tommy shakes his head. "Last time I tried that with you I lost money. No thanks, bro." Tommy stops what he's doing and looks over at his friend. "Besides, aren't those games like, illegal? And like, don't they take advantage of suckers?"

"I dunno," Paulo shrugs, "All I know is you gotta be first. If people are suckers, they're suckers. All I care about is me! I'll take the money if there's a chance. People can decide if they want to play or not."

Tommy finishes his work on the computer. He says to his friend, "Well, good luck or whatever, but leave me out of it. I don't want to be another sucker!" He sniffs and yawns. "So, are we gonna see a movie or what today?"

"Maybe later or something." Paulo replies, "I have to have a chat with my dad tonight about going out so late and stuff."

"Huh?" Tommy grimaces a bit, confused.

"Yeah," Paulo replies in a dismissive tone, "no big deal." He quickly changes the topic. "Hey, can I borrow forty bucks?"

Tommy frowns, "We just got paid, bro." Then he raises his eyebrows. "Don't tell me."

Paulo interrupts, "I'll pay you back when my airline game finishes. I just need it to pay my mom back, first."

Tommy exhales aloud and slouches his head forward. "Dude, when are you gonna learn?" He presumes what had probably happened to Paulo's paycheck. "Okay, okay, but at least stay a while and let's play this totally for real game I just got from our store!"

Tommy, smiling now, reaches for the 'Gran Turismo 3: A-Spec' case. Paulo nods happily in agreement, and he picks up one of the PlayStation 2 game controllers in response.

· · · • ● • · · ·

PAULO RETURNS HOME from Tommy's house after pretty much playing video games all Saturday afternoon. But he's made sure to get home before his dad arrived.

It is now 5:30 PM and everybody is home. Alejo is watching his favorite television show, Fear Factor. He never misses an episode. Paulo is in his own room watching the show COPS on television. Mary is busy preparing the table so they can eat dinner.

After a few minutes the table is ready. She walks towards her husband and says, "Al, dinner is ready." Then she walks toward the bottom of the stairs and says aloud, "Paulo it's dinner time!"

Alejo gets up from his reclining chair and starts walking to the dining table just as the house phone rings. He lifts the receiver on the phone and starts speaking with the caller. Paulo comes downstairs and is just about to sit when his cell phone rings. Now both men are talking while Mary is sitting patiently, ready for them to eat.

Alejo was very happy to hear his friend, Rick on the line. Rick is his mahjong buddy. They play mahjong all the time, especially on the weekends. "Pare (*My friend*) Rick, how are you?" Alejo happily greets him.

"Good, good pare. (*my friend.*)" Rick answers.

"Rick, what do we have? I was hoping you'd call because it's the weekend and somehow my hands are feeling itchy to shuffle something, you know like blocks or cards. And I don't know why I'm feeling lucky today." Alejo proclaims, teasing.

Both of them laugh, then Rick replies, "Well, that's why I'm calling because my cousin from Canada is here, and he wants to play mahjong. And there's only three of us. Your kumare (*female friend*) is working an early shift tomorrow and she wants to go to bed early." Rick is referring to his own wife.

"I see. I see. You know I can't pass this kind of invite. Do you want me to bring anything?" Alejo asks.

"No, you don't need to. We have a lot of food here. So just bring yourself here as soon as you can so we can start. The earlier the better!" Rick affirms.

Alejo happily accepts. "Okay, I will be there."

"Thank you! I see you then." Rick concludes.

Alejo hangs up the phone with a big smile on his face. He turns to face Mary. But before he can even say a word to his wife, she gives him a familiar look and hand gesture, *'Go!'* Mary already knows. Alejo walks over to the table and kisses her on the forehead.

"It will not be all night Hon, I promise." Alejo assures.

"Ay (*Oh*) Mr. Alejo Pineda, I am your wife, no? Since when do you go and play mahjong with your friends for only a couple of hours? I already know, it'll be all night 'til the morning comes." Mary says, rolling her eyes.

Alejo's only reply is a familiar expression on his face that Mary interprets as, *Okay, you're probably right.* Alejo checks to see if he has enough cash in his wallet to gamble with. He walks past Paulo, who is still talking on his mobile phone.

"Okay. I will be there." Paulo ends his call. Paulo had heard a few words from his father's phone conversation and assumes his dad had decided to go out for the evening. His dad's usual routine on a Saturday night. Paulo is relieved. *Good!* he thinks, because now his dad is going to play mahjong with his friends. This means the lecture for being irresponsible and whatever else, has been canceled.

Alejo pauses at the front door. "I'm leaving now. Wish me luck! Bye." Alejo gives a wave and smiles, leaving, almost in a hurry. Alejo can't wait to play mahjong with his good friends.

Mary and Paulo wish him good luck and wave in return.

"Are you leaving too?" Mary asks her son, assuming so.

"No, not right now, but I'll go and hangout with Tommy later." Paulo answers.

Mary is thinking how it's going to be a quiet night for her to just relax. She will have time now to catchup with her favorite teleserye (*television series*).

Paulo grins and turns his attention to his dear mom. "Mom," he asks her encouragingly, "would you come with me to the next Herbalife meeting?" Paulo continues, "I was just talking to my friend Alice who is an agent. She recently became a local distributor. She's moving up. Good chance to make money in this, I think."

"Son, I don't have time for that. I seldom have time to sell my Amway and Avon," Mary laughs. "And what other stuff have you been doing lately besides going to the casino, playing video games? Anything more productive, Paulo?" She inquires.

"Not really. Just the meeting that I told you about. I hope this will do me good, Mom." Paulo replies.

Mary and Paulo sit together and eat the delicious meal she has prepared. There's some small talk. And they share some lighthearted laughter talking about humorous situations involving their relatives abroad. Paulo smiles as he listens considerately to his mother sharing the latest gossip at work, too. Mary always appreciates the times her dear son spends with her, letting her talk about whatever is on her mind. Paulo helps his mother clear the dishes and soon after, he is in his car heading straight to another Native American casino in Rancho Mirage.

CHAPTER 6
IT'S LAST CALL

ALTHOUGH IT'S CROWDED, Paulo is able to quickly find a seat at one of his favorite slot machines, Wild Horses. The sound of ringing and chiming casino games fills his ears. In the distance, someone shouts for joy from winning a small jackpot. He hears laughter and people having conversations all around him. The vibe is good tonight, lots of energy. It feeds his need to gamble. He inserts $140 cash into the slot machine. Paulo sighs heavily and rubs his hands together quickly. *Time to get to business.* He can hardly wait for the machine to calculate his credits before he pushes the button to spin the reels.

The games begin. At the maximum $3 bet, it takes twelve spins before Paulo hits a row of three double horses on the single payline. His eyes see it coming just before the horses align together. The machine buzzing and blinking like it is actually alive and cheering for him. Paulo wins forty times his bet. He looks at his winnings in the display screen. In a short time, he has almost doubled the amount of money he brought with him. He considers taking all the money and going home. Maybe he shouldn't press his luck? Paulo continues to play.

Later, after almost five hours of playing, Paulo feels victorious. He is excited now because he has more than tripled the amount of money his mother and Tommy gave him. And instead of staying to press his luck further, he decides to leave with his winnings. It is difficult for him, but he finds the willpower to resist playing and exit the casino. He heads for the parking lot. Looking behind him once, he's thinking about changing his mind. But he leaves.

· · · · • • ● • • · · ·

PAULO IS HALFWAY home when he decides to get a drink to celebrate his winnings of sorts. He pulls into the driveway of a small, old dive bar named, Muscle Morgan's. There doesn't seem to be much activity. It is very late, but he feels he should stop.

Paulo is walking into the bar as a couple of people exit past him. The bar looks as if it is about to close. The bartender notices him enter and raises his voice to get Paulo's attention.

"Last call." He says, cleaning a beer glass.

Paulo nods and sits at the bar next to a skinny, scruffy looking white man holding a lit cigarette. There is a backpack on the floor next to him. Paulo notices his wrinkly, unshaven face hunched over his glass of Scotch-Whiskey on the rocks. The man pays no attention to Paulo's entrance, nor does he acknowledge Paulo as he takes a seat at the bar. The bartender slides an ashtray in front of the man and looks at Paulo.

"What can I get you?" The bartender points at Paulo. He is an older white man. Paulo notices and thinks the man is very muscular for his age. *Must be his bar*, Paulo reasons.

"Can I get a Budweiser?" Paulo politely asks. The bartender turns quickly to get him a bottle from the bar chiller.

Paulo looks around and notices he and the skinny man at the bar are the only patrons remaining. Paulo feels eerie for some unbeknownst reason. The quiet is distractingly unsettling. Music from a modern juke box in the corner of the bar is the only sound heard through the awkward quiet. The song, 'Bloodstone' by Judas

Priest is playing. Paulo taps his finger to the melody, listening to the song. He can clearly hear the lyrics.

I've been trying
There's no denying
It's sending me
Out of my mind...
I've seen reason
Change to treason
It's losing its sense
Of all kind...

The bartender slides the cold bottle of beer towards Paulo. The beverage stops right in front. "Let me know if you want another." The bartender nods, "But make it soon."

Paulo nods in acknowledgement. He glances at the man next to him again. The man is smirking, as if he just heard a dirty joke. He seems to be in his own world, not paying any attention to anything else. The man takes a sip of his drink and continues to smoke, staring at his glass. He looks like he is in deep thought.

Paulo stares at his beer. Now he is thinking deeply. Paulo thinks about his future. Everything his mother and father say to him comes to mind. He knows he should be living on his own and trying to find a better career. Yet, he is so very comfortable at home. *What's wrong with living at home a little longer?* he wonders. He will be able to save some money and move out, eventually. He and Tommy sometimes talk about getting an apartment together. Their own killer bachelor pad, they joke. *Maybe it's time*, Paulo considers.

"Joseph." A voice from behind Paulo startles him. He turns to look. "Nice to find you." The man says.

There are two men standing close to the bar. One of them has a smirk on his face. He is overweight with long black and gray hair, looking like an old rock star. The other man is younger. Cleanshaven head, very slim and taller than the guy that just spoke. Joseph, is half turned around with his back towards Paulo. Although Paulo can't see Joseph's face, he sees Joseph's cigarette smoke drifting above his head.

"Don't look so surprised." The overweight guy smiles, "Come on man." He chuckles, "You're staying at a hotel you sometimes use when you travel doing our business over here. And you and Beth once brought me here. It wasn't that hard, Joseph. Come on, man." He looks at his companion and they both laugh sarcastically. The man nods his head at Joseph, "Go figure." They chuckle again.

"It's last call." The bartender interrupts, "What are you having, gentlemen?"

The hefty man flicks his long black and gray hair from his face, looks at his companion and says, "Couple beers, any domestic is good." He nods and smiles at the bartender.

"What the hell you want, Gary?" Joseph inquires, coolly.

Gary and the other man laugh out loud. They are looking at each other and pointing at Joseph.

"What do I want, he says." Gary replies, still chuckling. "Joseph, you know what I want. We both know what you've got, and I just want to get things straightened out, man." He points at the table next to him. "Come on over here and take a seat. Let's have a little talk, Joseph. Let's be civilized gentlemen." More chuckles.

Paulo sees Joseph pick up the backpack. He watches him shuffle through the backpack for a moment. Then, Joseph sits up and coolly composes himself.

"Woah!" The bartender exclaims, standing perfectly still. He's holding two bottles of Budweiser, one in each hand. He's wide-eyed, gawking at Joseph.

"Shut up!" Joseph speaks clearly and intently. "Don't move." He quickly turns his head to look at his 'former' business associates. As he repositions himself on the barstool, Paulo sees the Glock 17C 9mm pistol Joseph is holding. Paulo's heart immediately starts to beat faster. His instincts tell him to run for the exit. But he remains frozen stiff with fear sitting on his barstool, not moving a muscle.

"Yo!" The cleanshaven man exclaims. "Put that down, man!"

"Shut up, Carl!" Joseph states, pointing the gun at the taller man. "Nobody fucking move!" Joseph glances quickly at Paulo. "You, kid." He nods at Paulo. "Come stand over here where I can see you all better." He points towards the bartender as he stands up. Paulo says nothing and quickly does exactly what Joseph wants, standing directly in front of the bartender on the other side of the bar.

"Let's talk about this, Joseph." Gary sincerely beseeches.

"Shut up!" Joseph commands again. "Now, everybody raise your fucking hands. Let me see your palms." Joseph starts to smile. He looks like he wants to laugh. As everyone put their hands up, Joseph states his demands. "The bartender and young fella here are gonna sit here nice and quiet while we drive away right now, together. And they're not gonna call anybody or do anything. Right?!" Joseph looks at the bartender. The man, still holding the beers in his raised hands, shakes his head fervently in acknowledgement.

Joseph snickers. "Good, good." Then he points the gun at Carl. "Turn around, Carl. And take your gun and put it on the table. Keep your back to me while you do it. I know you have one. You're always packing." Joseph says, snuffing his finished cigarette in the ashtray, while keeping close watch of his associates.

Carl does as Joseph has requested without saying a word. While turned around, he pulls a concealed Smith & Wesson .38 Special from the small of his back and places it slowly on the table next to him. Carl puts his hands up again.

Joseph smiles bigger. "I know you don't have nothing, Gary. You don't like guns."

"Yes, that's true." Gary responds quickly. "So, what are you going to do, Joseph? Shoot us right here? If you want a bigger share of the money or something..."

"No more talking!" Joseph interrupts with a raised voice. "Nobody needs to know shit about anything I'm doing here. I'll do the talking. And right now, I want you two fellas to walk out that door. We're going for a little drive, boys." Joseph starts chuckling. "Move it!" He gestures with the pistol towards the main entrance, scowling at Gary and Carl.

Gary and Carl start to slowly walk together, keeping their backs to Joseph. Their hands raised. They don't want any trouble. As they move, Joseph goes to the table and quickly puts the .38 revolver in his backpack. Then, he slings the backpack over his shoulder.

Joseph turns his head slightly and says to the bartender and Paulo, "This is business between me and my, uh, partners here. You don't need to get yourselves involved. Just pretend we were never here, gentlemen."

Joseph digs in his pocket with his free hand and retrieves some cash. He places it on the same table the gun was on. Then he walks away with the other men in front of him. He holds the Glock low by his side, pointed at the men in front of him the whole while. They quietly walk out the door. Only the music is heard again, the same song, Bloodstone.

Start to wonder
What's going under
And how many deals
Have been made...
How much longer will it take
For the world to see
We should learn to live
And simply let it be...
Bloodstone, bloodstone
Bloodstone, bloodstone...

Paulo and the bartender are staring at each other in shock.

They slowly lower their hands together and look at the main entrance. Neither moves from where they are standing, yet. It's as if they're both waiting for someone to tell them what to do next. They're completely stupefied.

· · · · • ● • · · · ·

OUTSIDE THE BAR it is very dark and there is nobody in sight. There are no cars on the small street. The parking lot only has three vehicles. One of those vehicles was a very clean, champagne-pearl, 1999 Plymouth Breeze. It was parked facing the exit. Joseph notices how it was parked and figures it was probably situated for a quick getaway, if necessary.

"You drive, Carl." Joseph commands, "Sit in front with him, Gary." He starts smiling again. Joseph doesn't have a car. He took a cab to the bar. This was very convenient. "Nice you drove, Gary."

They all get in Gary's Plymouth. Carl starts the engine and puts it into gear, asking, "Where are we going? Back to Vegas?"

Joseph laughs sarcastically. "No, no, no we're not going to Vegas! I've got better plans. Something more fun!" He gestures with the gun from the backseat. "Now listen. I want you to take the ten freeway east, to Palm Springs. Let's get going, fellas!"

Joseph certainly did have something else in mind. What he did not disclose was his plans to drive to the middle of the nearby desert and leave his associates out there in the dark. Somewhere far from the main highway. Joseph wants to put some distance between the two men and LAX where he will be heading for his flight to Brazil.

As the car moves towards the street edge, Gary starts to plead. "Joseph, please, let's be civilized. Come on, man. We can work something out. I'm sure we can come to a mutual agreement, man." He turns to look at Joseph, who is pointing his Glock right at him now.

"Turn around and keep your hands where I can see them." Joseph's tone is much more serious. "I'll shoot you both and take the car right now. I mean it." Then he presses the barrel onto the top of Carl's shoulder over the driver seat. "If you want to live tonight, you do as I say. Got it?" He cynically smiles. Joseph sits back, lights a cigarette and exhales cigarette smoke up to the car roof.

"Okay, okay." Carl promptly replies as he checks for traffic. He sees a 1991, midnight-blue, Buick Park Avenue approaching on their side of the street. Carl keeps his foot on the brake. "There's no need for anybody to get killed over this, man. Okay?" Carl turns his head towards Joseph in the rear seat. A calm tone in his voice. Gary also turns back to look at Joseph.

Gary is terrified. He's never seen Joseph act like this for as long as he had known him. He was certain Joseph would just fearfully concede and willingly come to an agreement as soon as they caught up with him. Gary was wrong. Joseph is consumed by greed.

During their conversation, Carl didn't notice that the Buick had changed lanes to the wrong side of the road. The driver, a fifty-five-year-old man, is the sole occupant of that vehicle. He had been out all evening drinking shots of Tequila with his work buddies. He's intoxicated, over three times the legal limit. He's driving erratically, the car is swerving the entire time.

All of a sudden, the Buick veers out of the wrong lane and turns directly towards the headlights of Gary's beautifully polished Plymouth. Carl turns forward to check again for traffic and immediately sees the bright headlights approaching directly for them.

Gary also sees the approaching vehicle, and screams, "Watch out! Watch out!"

·   ·   ·   •   ●   •   ·   ·   ·

BACK AT THE bar, Paulo picks up the money left by Joseph from the table and turns to look at the bartender, who is still standing in place. "There's two five-hundred-dollar bills here." Paulo says.

Suddenly, there is a terrific boom. Their eyes widen in alarm and they run towards the front entrance together.

They stop in their tracks as soon as they step outside. What they both see is simply, awful. In plain view is a mangled mess of contorted wreckage. Both vehicles are steaming and hissing. Oil and water are draining heavily on the ground from the engines. The Buick has stopped right at the entrance to the parking lot. It's compacted hood and engine compartment testifying the bleak outcome of the trauma-tizing force of impact. Carl's Plymouth has spun around onto the sidewalk, with twisted parts of exterior molding and shattered glass littered all around it. Paulo's mouth is agape. He doesn't know what to do. He's too scared to do anything.

The bartender puts a hand on Paulo's shoulder. "I'll call nine-one-one!" The man says and quickly runs back inside the bar. Paulo nods in response, eyes wide open.

Paulo walks cautiously closer to the wreck of the Buick. He really doesn't want to see anything. Paulo is very squeamish. As he gets closer, he leans to try and look at the car from the front. The crumpled hood is obscuring much of his view. He sees that the airbags have been discharged. But from where he stood, he could not see the driver. The reason Paulo can't see the driver is because the man was not wearing a safety belt. He is lying below the dashboard, out of sight.

Paulo continues slowly towards the impacted Plymouth. He reasons logically that this was the vehicle the three men were in. Paulo didn't remember seeing that car when he got to the bar. And from his point of view, it appeared to have been leaving the parking lot when it was violently struck. Although the parking lot and street on that side are not lighted very well, the devastation was crystal clear.

Paulo sees what he believes to be the taller man. Yes, it is Carl. He has been partially ejected from the driver side of the vehicle. His body is hanging halfway out the shattered window over the driver's door. He is motionless. Paulo chooses not to go closer and check on him. He is too afraid to. Then, he hears someone coughing.

It's Joseph. He is lying across the rear bench seat. Paulo goes around the back of the vehicle to the right rear passenger door. He sees Joseph is lying face up, head towards him. Paulo opens the door slowly. As he does, he sees what he thinks is Gary. He is face down, head forward over the top of the dashboard. His body has smashed into the front windshield. Paulo places his hand over his mouth as he seriously wants to vomit.

"Kid." A voice beckoned, coughing. "Hey, kid." Paulo looks down and notices Joseph is looking directly at him. It's obvious that he's been thrown around in the crash. His legs are awkwardly crossed away from him. His face and upper body, covered with blood and shards of auto glass. Paulo is unable to speak. He doesn't know what to do. He just stares at him. "My backpack." Joseph coughs. "Look in my backpack."

Paulo quickly spots the backpack lying on the floor of the vehicle close to Joseph's head. "We've called an ambulance. They're coming now." Paulo tries his best to sound brave, like he was in charge of the situation, to sound positive and helpful.

"No time for that." Joseph groans. "Reach in my backpack." He tries to raise his right arm a little and grimaces. "I want you to take it." Pointing his finger at Paulo.

"What are you talking about?" Paulo frowns, confused.

"Take the box before the cops come. They'll keep it and I don't want that to happen. I want you to have it. Better you have it than them. I'm giving it all to you now, kid." Joseph starts to smile, finding satisfaction in the thought of it.

"What? Oh, a box..." Paulo reaches into the backpack. He feels a velvet box underneath some clothes sitting on top of Carl's Smith &

Wesson .38 revolver. He retrieves what he thinks Joseph is asking for. "You want this, sir?" Paulo shows Joseph the closed jewelry case. "Is this what you're looking for?"

Joseph chuckles and coughs. He smiles greedily, and happily, although his present situation was quite grave. "Yes!" He spoke up, looking directly into Paulo's eyes. "Take it! And they will bring you great fortune!" He starts to laugh again, almost hysterically.

Paulo can't think why Joseph is carrying on so. *What's in the box?* He's curious. Paulo slowly opens the box. As the box reveals its precious contents to Paulo's anticipating eyes, Joseph begins to laugh louder. Paulo is now privileged a glorious eyeful of the Almasi Ya Kifo diamonds.

The exact moment Paulo looks at the bewildering jewels, he sees them glimmer. Almost as if, they did so purposefully, on cue. Paulo doesn't react for he is immediately entranced with what he's looking at. Something is taking over him. Some immediate uncontrollable desire that Paulo couldn't understand is building deep within his very soul.

"Yes." Joseph serenely responds. He could see within the young man's rapt gaze there was just a hint of a twinkle of the beautiful diamonds in Paulo's pupils. "Beautiful, aren't they?" He says just above a whisper. Joseph is enjoying this bewitching moment.

Paulo does not speak, or move. He only stares at the gems. Gazing deeply into them.

"Yes." Joseph giggles. He catches Paulo's attention saying, "Take them and go!"

Paulo shifts his gaze from the stunning diamonds to Joseph, still bleeding and lying severely injured on the rear bench seat. Saying nothing, Paulo methodically closes the case, stands up, and turns around without blinking an eye. He is bewitched.

Paulo hears Joseph as he begins to walk away. "They're yours. You keep them now, kid." Joseph coughs and gurgles. His breathing is becoming shallow. His arm is lying limp next to his gun on the car floor as he says, "Almasi Ya Kifo." He smiles and begins to chuckle a little. Then suddenly, he is motionless. Joseph Ashe is deceased, his eyes open in a lifeless gaze up to the car ceiling.

Paulo calmly walks over to his parked 1990 white Nissan Sentra 2-door coupe. He opens the car and gently places the diamonds on the passenger seat. He stares at the closed jewelry case, emotionless. Not a word.

· · · • ● ● ● · · ·

"Let's talk." The bartender beckons from the bar entrance. "Let's get our story straight before the cops get here." He motions quickly for Paulo to come to him.

"I'm Morgan. This is my bar." He says as Paulo walks towards him, "What's your name young man?"

"My name is Paulo, sir." Paulo responds, as Morgan puts a friendly hand on Paulo's shoulder. In the near distance, the sirens of fast approaching emergency response vehicles can now be heard.

Paulo and Morgan tell their separate witness accounts to the police that had responded to the accident scene. They both give the same statement as they had agreed upon. There was not a single mention of the brandished gun. No mention of the precarious conversation and hostility that took place. No mention of the money left behind on the table. They simply state that a couple guys came in and met another man that was already there. They had a few drinks, then they all left together. Next, there was a terrible accident outside. Their stories were corroborated. The police aren't interested in anything else. Only the discernable smell of liquor on the deceased driver of the Buick drew the attention of the police now.

CHAPTER 7
THIS WILL SOLVE ALL MY PROBLEMS

MARY WAS AWAKE at 6:00 AM this beautiful Sunday morning. She sits on the side of the bed facing her altar, reciting her morning Catholic devotional. Alejo is still sound asleep. He returned home not too long ago after playing mahjong with his friends almost the entire night. Mary is careful not to disturb him while she silently finishes her prayers.

Mary heads downstairs to the kitchen to prepare breakfast for her beloved family. She has just started making coffee when she suddenly hears the front door open. She immediately stops what she is doing and looks towards the door. To her astonishment Mary sees Paulo walking in.

She looks at the oven clock and says with a slight raised voice, "Are you serious? Is this going to be your weekend routine? To come home at this time?" Mary points at the clock as Paulo enters the kitchen. "AND don't tell me Paulo, you came from the casino, again!" She gestures *'no'* with the same pointed finger at him.

"No, no mom. I was driving home when I witnessed a deadly crash. It was a horrible head on. I had to give my statement to the police. Look, I'm all shaken up." Paulo replies as he stretches out his arms shaking them over-exaggeratingly.

"Oh my God, so sorry. I'm glad you're okay. Oh Diosko salamat (*oh Lord, thank you*) for protecting my son. Mary emotionally utters as she hugs her son dearly. She pats his chest and squeezes his arms in her ritualistic way, as if making sure she's not hugging a ghost. Paulo smiles.

"I'm sure you were scared to see all that. Do you need to see a doctor?" Mary questions sincerely.

"No mom, I think I'm okay. I'll let you know how I do in the next couple days." Paulo replies, "I'm going to my room now to rest."

"Do you need me to make you something before you go upstairs? Or do you need water?" Mary asks him.

"Water is fine mom, thank you." He quietly says.

Mary takes a bottled water from the fridge and hands it to her dear son. Paulo takes it, nodding his head to express his humble gratitude.

"I'll see you later Mom." Paulo waves his hand holding the bottled water.

"Okay anak (*son*). Shower first so you feel fresh and able to fall asleep." Mary suggests, imparting her parental wisdom.

Paulo goes upstairs, closing and locking his door. He had concealed the box so his parents couldn't see it. The velvet case is cleverly balled up in a jacket he had in his car. He uncovers the pretty black box containing the precious stones. Then Paulo pulls the money out of his pocket that he happily split with the bar owner, Morgan. It was Morgan's generous suggestion to split the cash, an effort to reassure Paulo's confidence and silence.

He places the crisp $500 bill next to the black velvet case on his bed. Then he opens the box. Paulo is mesmerized as he gazes at the diamonds. He knows they are probably worth a lot of money. He wonders how much money he could get for them.

"This is it! Shit!" He says to himself. "Yes! Now you see what happens when you're lucky. This must have happened to me for a reason. This will solve all my problems. I can finally move out and buy my own house. I will spoil myself with a couple new cars and, maybe buy my parents new cars too. I'll pay in cash! That will impress them. I will pay my credit card bills and pay my parents whatever money I owe them. I'm sure my dad will be happy and proud of me! Oh, maybe I'll take a month vacation somewhere I've never been? And I will still have lots of money left. I think I'm set for life baby! Yeah!" He fist-pumps the air. "See what happens when you're lucky?!"

The sudden sound of his mother's footsteps going to her bedroom startles him. Paulo immediately closes the box. He thinks for a second where to hide it. He has an idea. Opening his closet, Paulo puts the case of priceless diamonds in an empty shoebox, a satisfactory, temporary hiding spot until he can think of a better place. He snatches the $500 bill off the bed and puts it back in his pocket.

Paulo lays down and rests his head on his favorite Bart Simpson pillow. His mind is contemplating idea after idea. He's thinking how and where he's going to sell his diamonds. Not being able to sleep, he decides to take a shower as his mother had suggested.

Mary had gone upstairs to wake her husband for breakfast. Not long after, Alejo joins her at the table. Mary shares what Paulo said to her husband. Alejo is relieved knowing their only son was unharmed and he was in his room safe, sleeping now.

Paulo finishes showering and lays down on his bed again. He is still thinking about how he is going to sell his diamonds. He closes his eyes for a couple minutes then, suddenly his Auntie Elvira comes into his mind.

"Auntie Elvie!" Paulo opens his eyes wide. "Shit, that's right, my auntie, how can I forget?" He says to himself, "Hmm, but I wonder if she's in L.A. and if she still has the same number. I haven't talked to her for a while. I wonder if mom knows."

Listening carefully, Paulo can hear his parents talking at the dining table. He quickly gets dressed and hurries downstairs to join them. His mother and father are surprised to see him.

"Can't sleep?" Mary asks with a concerned look.

"No." Paulo answers. "Good morning, dad." He greets his father as he grabs a plate for breakfast.

"Good morning. So, what is this accident you witnessed?" Alejo inquires, as Paulo takes a seat at the table. "Head on? Whew! Whoever caused it were probably intoxicated. These idiots, I don't know why they like to drink and drive. That's why, Paulo don't come home after midnight because nothing good happens after midnight. See what you just witnessed?"

"Yes, dad I know." Paulo begins eating his food.

"Ahem, speak for yourself too, Al." Mary coolly remarks.

"Well, I'm smarter than that, Mary. I just go and play. I don't drink and drive. But ah, anyway Paulo, your mom and I are thankful it was not you and that you're okay." Alejo squeezes his son's shoulder firmly.

Alejo excuses himself from the table to go and watch some TV. He wants to watch the NFL games this Sunday. Because, he had made a very considerable wager on the Minnesota Vikings versus the Chicago Bears game later that morning. He bet on the Bears to win, and there was a generous additional bonus if they did so with a 7-point spread. Alejo regularly participated in a large pool that mostly consisted of his local Post Office coworkers. They always bet for money on just about any televised sports event. And he hardly ever missed an opportunity to join the fun.

Paulo turns towards his mom and asks, "Mom, is auntie Elvie in town and does she have the same number?"

Alejo hears his son's question, and reacts as if he were going to battle stations after hearing the Klaxon of an impending divebombing airstrike.

"Why in the world are you asking about Lesbo? Do you need her for something, huh Paulo?" He glowers at his son.

"I'm just asking because I haven't heard from her for a while. She's family, dad and, I'm just wondering how she's doing. Geeze!" Paulo replies with a stern voice, while slowly shaking his head.

"Well, she is in town and has the same number." Mary calmly answers, mixing her coffee with cream the way she likes.

"She's still with Gigi and living in the same place?" Paulo asks very curiously.

"Yup." Mary nodded, still stirring her coffee.

Alejo is quiet, listening to their conversation. Then he exclaims, "Better be just that, Paulo. I know that Lesbo very well. I don't trust her and she's not a good influence!"

"Al, stop being judgmental and saying unkind words. She has a NAME, for God sake. You are talking about my sister who helped us a lot when we didn't have anything. She helped you coming here from the Philippines, my God! What's wrong with you, Alejo Pineda?" Mary retorts.

Paulo quietly gets up and takes his empty plate into the kitchen. He waves to his mom, and goes upstairs to his room, closing and locking the door behind him, again.

Paulo takes the pretty black velvet case from the closet and opens it. Looking again at the sparkling diamonds, he becomes even more eager to sell them. He can't wait to have all the money in his hands. He snaps the lid close, grabs his mobile phone and begins to search for his auntie Elvie's number.

"Aha, there you are!" Paulo says aloud when he finds her number. He makes the call.

· · · · ● ● ● · · ·

ELVIRA 'ELVIE' CHAVEZ and her longtime partner, Gina 'Gigi' Alba are just finishing a quiet brunch at a trendy restaurant along Pacific Coast Highway, not far from their home. They had attended an enriching morning service at The Queen of Living Catholic Church in the City of Orange, earlier.

Elvira's phone starts ringing. She looks to see who is calling and is surprised to see Paulo's name on her phone ID screen. "Hello stranger." She answers, smiling.

"Auntie Elvie, how are you? Long time no talk and no see." Paulo happily replies. He's smiling, anticipating his plan to become wealthy in motion and quickly coming together now.

"I know. I thought you've forgotten me already anak (*son*)." Elvie teases with a slight frown.

"Forgotten? Nah. No way! You're my best auntie, auntie!" Paulo says sincerely.

"Yeah, yeah, yeah, okay. You're fooling me again. So, what made you call? Is everything okay?" Elvie abruptly questions.

"Yes, but since you asked, I want to see you tomorrow after work." Paulo is direct, cutting to the chase.

"For what, are you in trouble?" Elvie curiously asks.

"No! I want to see you because I need to show you something! Can we meet at Redlands Park, tomorrow after work?" Paulo has just about demanded their meet by his tone of voice. The open case of sparkling diamonds is in his hands. A surge of confidence manifests within him as he gazes upon them. It is that same secure feeling he experienced when he first looked upon them.

"Kiddo, you're lucky. We will be that side of town tomorrow to meet one of my gold exchange reps. So, what are you thinking, five to five-thirty?" Elvie asks.

"Perfect! Yes, talking about luck, I am very lucky!" Paulo boasts, fist-pumping the air as before. "I'll see you tomorrow then, adios (*bye*)." Paulo ends the call quickly.

"B..." Elvie doesn't even finish saying goodbye to her nephew when Paulo ends the call. She looks at Gigi, confused. "Hmm, that's weird." She murmurs.

"Okay ka lang beh (*Are you okay babe*)?" Gigi asks.

"Oo (*Yes*), I'm okay. We are going to see Paulo tomorrow at the park after our meeting with Liv. He said he's going to show me something." Elvie replies and shrugs her shoulders.

She takes the last sip of her tall Bloody Mary cocktail and asks Gigi if their bill has been paid. Gigi nods while gathering their belongings. She positions a wheelchair alongside Elvie. Using a stylish walking cane to assist her, Elvie transfers herself from her seat and then into their car. A few minutes later, they are on their way home.

CHAPTER 8
YOU GUYS ARE CRAZY!

T 5:10 PM the next day, Elvie and Gigi drive into the park. They find a good parking space that is close to the ramp where Gigi can easily push Elvie's wheelchair around. There aren't many people at the park, and no one was close by their spot. They look around, but there's no sign of Paulo just yet. Gigi gets out of their tall black SUV and retrieves the wheelchair. Using her cane, Elvie slowly gets out on her own and sits in her wheelchair. Gigi then rolls her to the ramp to the small private pavilion next to them.

Within a couple minutes, Paulo arrives and parks next to their SUV. Paulo quickly shuts off the engine and grabs the jewelry box from the glove compartment and places it in his PacSun backpack to conceal his business and intentions from any passersby. He looks at himself in the rearview mirror and smiles self-assuredly. Paulo gets out of his car and walks towards the pavilion where he sees Elvie and Gigi sitting patiently.

He kisses them both. "Hello beautiful aunties, how are you guys?" He's so excited. "My God, it's been a while! But seems like nothing has changed between the two of you. You both look good! Thank you for meeting up with me."

The two women smile. Elvie quips, "Good to see you too anak (*son*) but just so you know, I didn't like how you ended your call to me yesterday."

Gigi looks at Paulo and shrugs her shoulders in response. Paulo looks towards the ground, slightly taken aback.

Elvie continues. "So, what is it that you want to show me? It sounded like an emergency."

Paulo smiles cheerfully again at his aunties. "Do you still have contact with those diamond traders auntie Elvie?" Paulo earnestly enquires.

Elvie and Gigi look at each other, puzzled.

"Yes," Elvie pauses, "and why the sudden concern about what I do, Paulo?" She looks at him inquisitively.

Paulo reaches into his backpack. It was all he could do to contain the building exhilaration inside him. And with great anticipation, he presents the black velvet box to Elvie.

"Here is why. Take it and have a good look." His tone of voice is insistent. "Help me to sell them auntie but, gotta be the highest bidder. And I promise we will split it eighty-twenty." He points at himself first, then points at them, articulating unquestionably who gets what part of the share.

Elvie and Gigi stare at the case for a moment. Then they look at each other and, simultaneously return their attention to Paulo. Elvie takes the box from Paulo's hand. Elvie has purveyed many precious stones and is considered an expert by many of her associates in the diamond industry. She can look at the cut of a diamond, or the way its radiance presented itself, along with many other industry-learned standards and, identify where the gem was probably geographically from. She could accurately estimate what buyers would pay for certain exquisite gems. And now she held Paulo's fortuitist black velvet diamond case in her hands. But, for some unbeknownst, deep-down uncertainty, she began to slowly, almost cautiously, open it.

It only takes her a second to recognize the telltale crystalline appearance and notice their unique legendary radiant signature shape and cut. Suddenly, she snaps the case closed.

"Almasi Ya Kifo! Pucha (*Damn*). Sa'n mo kinuha, sa'n mo kinuha? *Where did you get them, where did you get them?*" She is nothing less than frantic, her voice rising and eyes wide open. Her hands start to tremble with absolute fear. Elvie is so terrified she thrusts the diamonds back into Paulo grasp. "Hindi ko nakita, hindi ko Nakita (*I didn't see them, I didn't see them*)!" Elvie repeats to herself in an unequivocally disturbed manner. She wants no part of what she is seeing, Paulo's cursed Mother lode of diamonds. Not even realizing, she grabs her cane and hooks Paulo by the arm to draw him closer to her.

Then she pulls him by his shirt, demanding him, "Tell me I didn't see those!"

Paulo is absolutely dumbfounded. He can't do anything but repeat what Elvie has just said. "You didn't see those."

Elvie lets him loose. She notices Gigi is also very flustered to see the exposed diamonds. "You didn't see those!" Elvie demands directly at Gigi.

"I didn't see those." Gigi repeats. "Ano ba ang nangyayari sa batang 'to (*What is happening with this kid*)?" Gigi asks of Elvie.

"I don't know, but obviously he doesn't know what these diamonds do to you. No wonder he was acting weird yesterday." Elvie nods in Paulo's direction as she talks to her loving and caring lifetime partner. "Because these diamonds were controlling and consuming him!"

Paulo is listening, but is confused. In his mind, these women are just freaking out over something stupid. Some beautiful stones are *controlling and consuming* him? Then he blurts out, "So are you going to help me or what?"

Elvie and Gigi gawk at him in obvious disbelief answering together in unison, "NO!"

Elvie signals Gigi to wheel her back to their car. She points at Paulo with her cane and says, "Give those back to where you got them from Paulo, or you'll die. I mean it!"

Paulo's not happy. This is not the reception he had expected or wanted, being the owner of the priceless gems. He's angry about what he has just heard from his auntie.

"Ahhh! You guys are crazy! I'm going to find somebody to help me. Thanks, but no thanks." He waves his hand dismissively at them, then rushes off without saying goodbye.

"I've warned you about them, Paulo. Remember, I ate more rice than you." Elvie reiterates while Gigi pushes her towards their car.

Paulo clearly heard what Elvie said, but he doesn't care. He drives away in a hurry. Elvie and Gigi both shake their heads. They simply can't believe that Paulo would not take heed and listen to sensible advice. Their drive back home was long and quiet.

CHAPTER 9
YOU KEEP THEM NOW, KID

PAULO IS THINKING as he drives home. He can't believe his auntie suggested to get rid of the prized diamonds. *Why would I do that? These are priceless, I know they are!* Paulo shakes his head. He decides to hold onto them for a while until he finds someone else to help him sell them. Or perhaps, Elvie will come to her senses and change her mind. She should consider the huge profits these will bring her, too.

"She just needs some time to think about it, and I'll talk some sense into her." Paulo smiles, greedily contemplating his next plan of action. Then he remembers what Joseph had said to him, *"Take it! And they will bring you great fortune!"*

"Yes!" Paulo says aloud, "These are my lucky diamonds! They will bring me a fortune!" His eyes widen as he grips the steering wheel tighter. "And he gave them to me!" The young man smiles, thinking about how fortunate he was to be there at the right time when Joseph Ashe gave them to him. The last thing Paulo remembered Joseph saying was *"They're yours. You keep them now, kid."*

Paulo hadn't stopped to consider that he received them from a man being chased and accosted by his partners that he had originally betrayed, and obviously ran away from. He got them from a man that was just involved in a fatal accident, bleeding all over while handing the diamonds to him. He hadn't given that part any thought. Paulo's lust for money is completely consuming him now.

Paulo considers testing the meritorious attributes of the diamonds. He looks at his backpack and comes up with an idea. He heads to Highland, to the nearest Native American casino, and less than half an hour later he is sitting down at his favorite Wild Horses slot machine. His backpack is down at his feet with the straps wound around his ankles to anchor it. He wants his lucky stones to be near him at all times. Paulo is holding the money he split with Morgan. His fingers tingle with anticipation of the glorious prospects ahead this evening. He slides the $500 bill into the ticket voucher bezel.

The gambling machine springs alive with a vibrant digital noise, as if it were saying, *where have you been my love?* Paulo smirks as he watches the credits rapidly counting up on the video display. The sound of ringing and chiming distant machines are heard as he presses the play maximum bet button. With great expectation, he leans forward and rubs his hands together vigorously as the reels begin to spin. And the games begin.

Something extraordinary happens. The very first spin yields a row of three triple horses aligned together on the payline. The machine buzzes and the lights flash as if it were seriously malfunctioning. Instead, it's announcing a jackpot winner! Paulo has just won $7,500 dollars on a single spin $3 bet.

Paulo pumps his first into the air in delight and looks around him. It's not very busy in that section of the casino and he's the only person sitting in that row of machines. Nevertheless, he celebrates his success.

"Yes!" He laughs and does a little dance in his chair.

A cashier walks up to him. "Congratulations!" She acknowledges as she put her hand on the slot machine. "Sir, I need to reset this machine, please." She smiles, holding a large set of keys on a wide keyring.

"Oh, okay." Paulo obliges, trying to move aside. He almost trips, forgetting about the backpack straps around his feet. The cashier politely thanks him as he awkwardly moves out of the way. She hands Paulo his winning ticket voucher from the machine and wishes him good luck.

He looks around, considering whether to try his luck on another slot machine. Maybe hitting this jackpot was just a one-time occurrence? He decides to test his hypothesis and see if he could win, again.

He has only taken a few steps when he notices another slot machine that he just HAS to play. He sits downs at a row of Double Diamonds slots. Paulo inserts the ticket voucher and watches as the machine counted the credits. He's pleased with how long it's taking for all his credits to show, and the time it takes for the machine to ready itself for play.

And again, he presses the $3 maximum bet button to spin the reels. The machine chimes a little jingle as the handsome diamond icons and various other symbols spin to the tune.

Then, his eyes widen in disbelief as the double diamond icons all align together. And suddenly, this machine also starts buzzing and blinking like the other slot he'd just won on. Paulo almost falls out of his chair as he sees he has hit another jackpot! He has just won another $7,500 dollars on a single spin $3 bet.

The same cashier that had helped him hadn't gone very far away when she hears the familiar sound of another jackpot payout. She turns around to see the same gentleman, Paulo sitting there.

"Wow! You're really lucky tonight! I've never seen this before! Wow!" The cashier smiles as Paulo laughs with joy. He remembered to move the backpack from underneath him this time, as he moves out of her way.

She hands him the winnings voucher, and he thanks her with a $10 tip this time. She gratefully thanks the young man and wishes him good luck, again.

It is obvious at least to him now that the diamonds must bring good luck. "Elvie is crazy." He scoffs.

He sits back down and retrieves his prized gems out of the backpack. Paulo barely opens up the case, sneaking a peek at his diamonds. He can see them sparkle beautifully in the crack of the opening. Smiling contentedly, Paulo thinks of what to do next. He wonders if he should stay. But if he keeps winning, security might want to get into his business and know what is going on. How is it he keeps winning, they may demand. Too much attention, Paulo considers. He thinks about coming back tomorrow. But he decides to go to another casino to further test his hypothesis of sorts. He wants to keep gambling. He wants more money. Paulo cashes out and leaves.

· · · • • ● • • · ·

AFTER DRIVING ANOTHER half hour, Paulo walks into the Native American casino in the Rancho Mirage area. He notices an automated electronic roulette wheel game near him. He sits down and inserts a crisp $500 bill into the awaiting currency bezel. He selects a maximum wager of $100 and puts the entire amount on 0, green to win. Pressing the spin button, he activates the game. The wheel spins quickly around and the ball is immediately discharged into play. Paulo watches and listens to the sound of the ball rounding the rotor. Suddenly, the ball bounces into the pockets and comes to an abrupt stop. He can't believe what he is seeing! The ball is resting in the 0, green pocket. Paulo smiles as the wager display shows WIN $3,500.

"Nothing can stop me!" He says bluntly, feeling invincible. "I'm keeping the diamonds, and nobody else can have them! They're mine!"

Paulo snickers, imagining achieving wealth beyond his dreams. He hastily retrieves his voucher from the collect ticket slit. He has another idea.

Paulo plants himself down at the Blazing Sevens slot machine, in the high-roller section. After securing the backpack underneath him, he makes himself more comfortable. Then, he methodically inserts cash and voucher equaling the entire amount of money he has won tonight, $18,500 into the ready and willing ticket bezel. He sneers at the game machine thinking; *I'm going to take everything you have!*

"Give it all to me. Time to pay up, bitch!" He laughs. Paulo looks around at the few people that are there. If only they knew. If only they had what he possesses, prosperity beyond imagination. He pressed maximum bet 3 coins, totaling $300.

To his complete surprise, the first spin yields nothing. No problem. He tries again, maximum bet. Nothing. He spins the reels again. Nothing aligns on the payline, not one icon. And twenty spins later, Paulo is now dumbfounded. Every spin has yielded nothing. He takes a deep breath, then exhales heavily. He notices his credits. The display is showing $11,600 remaining. *What's happening? I'm supposed to win!*

"I probably hit a dry spot of my winning right now." Paulo shrugs. "I should probably try again tomorrow."

He decides to leave with the remainder of his jackpots. Paulo gets up and heads for the exit.

Feeling hungry, Paulo decides to stop at the 24-hour grill inside the casino. After eating a hotdog, fries, and a Diet Coke, he heads outside to go to his car. Paulo stops just as he is about to open the door, and he turns around.

"Maybe I was just playing the wrong game." He says aloud. "I should go back and at least try again." He goes back inside.

By 2:00 AM, Paulo has just about gambled away all the money in his possession at the casino. He is baffled. He is angry. *What's happening, these are my lucky diamonds!* He rubs his head vigorously over and again. He's feeling defeated now. Paulo looks at the credits on the Cleopatra video slots he is now playing. The balance shows $26 and 50 cents. He digs in his pocket for more cash. His pockets are empty. His last voucher is in the machine, and it represents all the cash he has to his name right now.

Paulo shakes his head. He has spent the last several hours playing, going from machine to machine. He tried almost every machine in the casino. He even played the automated roulette game again. But the little white ball didn't land on a single number he placed a bet on.

Paulo is frowning. *I just don't understand.* He decides to leave again. *Then again, maybe I should get some cash from the ATM?* He tried to think how much money was in his emergency savings that his mother had setup for him when he was a young kid. He's never used it, and only thought about it, right now. He never felt so desperate, is why.

"I should really try and win all that money back." He says to himself, "I know the diamonds will help me do it. I just need to go to another casino."

Suddenly, the casino lights go out. Only the illumination of the machines running on separate power are dimly lighting the casino floor area. There are a few surprised gasps, then the emergency lights quickly come on. Paulo can hear someone with a raised voice in the distance.

"Everyone, exit the building, please. We are experiencing a blackout. Please make your way to the main exit, thank you!"

Paulo makes his way towards the exit. He can hear and see a few other people also gathering their things to leave. As he walks out to his car, he's thinking maybe he should just call it a night and get some rest. *Oh well, at least I have the diamonds. It's only money. I can get more and try again.*

"Tonight, was just a test. I know I can make a killing winning with these diamonds. I may not have to sell them after all. I just need to figure out their winning cycle is all." Paulo says convincingly to himself and nods.

Paulo makes it home safely and goes inside to his room without waking up his parents. He thinks about how he should probably leave the casino next time as soon as the winning ceases. He is convinced there must be a window of opportunity that exists. *Just like when the slots are loose.* He had to figure out when that moment was and when the fortune diamonds would be paying him. He gives that prospect serious thought and falls asleep while looking at his backpack and its wonderous contents.

CHAPTER 10
YOU HAVE SOMETHING THAT BELONGS TO FRIENDS OF MINE

B Y THE TIME Paulo gets up Tuesday morning to eat breakfast both his parents have already left for work. He fixes himself a bowl of cereal and sits down in the kitchen to eat. He takes the first mouthful when suddenly he hears his mobile phone ringing upstairs in his bedroom. Paulo races upstairs just in time to answer it.

It's Jacqueline calling to update him on the progress of the Ponzi scheme game and his 'investment' as she had before. Only this time, Paulo elects to cash out. Paulo wants the cash he has accumulated so he can gamble at the casino. Jacqueline says she will be happy to drop by his work and give him his profits. The call ends quickly.

Paulo is happy he will have more money to gamble with. He skips like a little kid and is about to go back downstairs when his mobile phone rings again. He picks up the phone and sees there's no name or number identification on the phone display. Simultaneously, the bedroom lights start flickering. *What?* He looks around and answers the call.

There is a solemn voice of a man on the line. "You have something that belongs to friends of mine. We've been watching you, that is, my friends have."

"Who is this?" Paulo grimaces. "Is this the police?"

"No. You are not in trouble from them or us. We just want to help you return something that you have."

"Who's this?!" Paulo's eyes shifted. The tone of his voice sounded much like his father just then.

"I am Chief Amitola. You can say, I am a contact person."

"Police Chief, what?!"

"No, not the police. I am part of the Paiute…"

"Ahh!" Paulo interrupts agitatedly. "This is prank call!" He ends the call abruptly and turns off his phone. Paulo has an idea what's going on. "Okay Elvie, now you're joking around!"

. · · · • ● • · · ·

Paulo is a little tired from staying up late the previous night, but he's excited to get to work because Jacqueline will be stopping by with his money. "More money for me to gamble with!" He taps on the steering wheel to the tune of the Smooth Criminal cover by Alien Ant Farm, playing on the radio.

He's in the left turning lane, about to proceed as the traffic light turns green. The vehicles on his side of the road start to move forward, then suddenly stop. As Paulo slowly moves forward, the driver of one of the cars next to him blasts his horn. Then Paulo sees a large silver 2001 Dodge dually truck approaching the intersection from his right side. It starts screeching and swerving. Its driver is accelerating instead of stopping to try and beat the red light. The truck veers past Paulo, missing his car by inches. The truck doesn't stop. The driver oblivious as he speeds away.

"Whew! That was close!" Paulo exclaims in relief. "Good thing I have my lucky diamonds!" He pats his backpack and drives on.

. · · · • ● • · · ·

AT MEGABUSTER VIDEO, Paulo is having a pleasant day working with his coworkers and friends. Tommy is there, making jokes as usual to help pass the time. Jacqueline arrives and, after renting a few videos for her kids, she hands him an envelope with $360 cash in it. His payout from the Ponzi game.

Paulo is having lunch in the tiny breakroom when Karen walks in.

"Hey Paulo." Karen smiles. She sits next to Paulo as he eats Taco Bell that Tommy brought in during the lunch run. "Got a second?"

Paulo nods eagerly, swallowing the last bite of his taco supreme. He clears his throat and reaches for his Diet Coke.

"Sure, Karen. What's up?" Paulo is always excited when Karen comes to talk to him, even though it's usually a favor regarding something that is work related. He's hoping that maybe, just maybe, he will get the nerve to ask her out this time. He tries to think of something they can go out and do together this weekend. He's thinking about asking her. He knows she's still single and not seeing anyone.

"Hey," Karen says, "my friend's friend is a DJ at the Rumjungle in Las Vegas." She squints trying to remember. "I think the club is in the Mandalay Bay. Anyway, a bunch of us are going this weekend. If you're interested, why don't you meet up with us?" She smiles at him encouragingly.

"Huh?" Paulo wonders what the hell just happened. *Did she just ask me out right now?* He is pleasantly thunderstruck. Just then, another coworker calls her name from the store.

"Anyway, you can ask Tommy, but I know he is supposed to work this coming weekend." Karen says as she gets up. "It should be fun! Hope to see ya." She nods and smiles at him.

"Okay, sure I'll think about it. Thanks Karen!" Paulo enthusiastically replies as she smiles again and walks out the breakroom door.

CHAPTER 11
YO! LOOK OUT!

PAULO IS ON his way home after work. He stops at a local market to get some things his mom had called to ask him to pick up. While shopping for the grocery items, Paulo is busy thinking. He wants to meet Karen in Las Vegas. Paulo can't wait to tell his mother about Karen talking to him and asking him to meet with her and her friends there. Mary knows he has had a crush on Karen for a while. Paulo also thinks about asking his mom for some extra money so he can treat Karen to a nice dinner.

Then, he has another thought. He entertains the idea of taking the diamonds with him so he can gamble on the Las Vegas strip. *Brilliant!* Whenever he starts to win, he figures he can just move on to the next casino. But first, he needs to figure out the winning cycle.

"Yes!" He snaps his fingers, excitingly contemplating everything. Paulo goes through the checkout line, picking up the grocery bags quickly to leave. As he's walking towards the exit, he hears someone raise their voice. He turns to see who it is.

"Sir, your wallet! Sir!" A grocery clerk is walking quickly towards him. The clerk gives Paulo his wallet and smiles politely. "You left it at the register."

"Oh my, thank you!" Paulo replies embarrassingly.

Paulo walks outside. He is looking down at the pavement, thinking about things again. Then Elvie comes into his mind. He is seriously thinking about calling her and asking if she can lend him money, too. That way, when he returns from Las Vegas with lots of money, she will believe him. He is going to convince her it is best for him to keep the lucky diamonds. And she needs to help him travel so he can win at different casinos, maybe around the world. They will form a gambling partnership.

"That's what I'll do!" Paulo says aloud.

Suddenly, Paulo hears the loud blare of a motorcycle air horn. He gasps and freezes in place. Paulo looks up to see an Indian Scout 100 motorbike stopped right next to him. The rider, a burly man wearing a black, World War II German army style pointed helmet, is shaking his head at him. The man slowly steers around Paulo. Then, keeping his eyes on Paulo, he revs the motor and drives off. Paulo continues walking towards his car. *My wallet, and now this. Good thing the diamonds are watching after me!*

· · · • ● ● • · · ·

AFTER HAVING DINNER with his parents, Paulo tells his parents he and Tommy are going to meet up at one of their favorite sports bar hangouts to have a few beers. But what Paulo really does is drive out to the Native American Casino in Coachella, a little more than an hour away from home.

He parks near the main entrance so he wouldn't have far to walk before thinking twice about leaving after he won his money. He wanted to lessen the temptation to keep playing as much as he can. He looks at the diamonds for motivation before walking inside the casino. A warm reassuring emotion coddles him as he gazes deep into the mysterious precious stones. A part of Paulo just wants to remain there sitting and looking at them. They just, make him feel good.

Paulo counts his money. He has over $480, including some money his mom gave him to go to Las Vegas this coming weekend.

He is ready. And a few minutes later, he is back at it, again. He is sat down at one of the Triple Diamond Deluxe progressive slot machines in a row not far from the main entrance. He puts all his cash bills into the machine, clasps his hands together and rubs them vigorously. *Okay here we go.* He takes a deep breath and exhales slowly.

The first maximum $3 bet spin stopped quickly, showing three single bars in a row on the payline. The machine chimed an abrupt jingle indicating a winning spin of 30 times the bet. Paulo smiles amusingly. He pulls the handle and the reels spin again. The next spin stops showing a row of triple bars. Another slightly longer winning jingle this time. And he spins the reels again. Then, all three triple diamonds align right before his eyes. The shiny machine starts buzzing and flashing crazily. It's a progressive jackpot win.

"Yes!" Paulo smiles at the slot machine, "Oh, it's a progressive jackpot, too! Yes, very nice!" He looks up to see the progressive jackpot payout of $2,500. "Awe," he frowns, "man, I should have played on a row with a bigger pot!" He shrugs his shoulders.

After the cashier visits and pays him, Paulo is thinking about leaving the casino and going home. He wants to stick to his plan and have some money to gamble with in Las Vegas.

Then again. "Maybe just one more time to double it. I want more money!" Paulo says, starting to look determined.

Paulo is sitting at the Double Diamonds slot in the high-roller section now. And, just as he is about to put all his money in the machine, it shuts down. The machine goes completely dark. Paulo leans back and grimaces. He looks around and discovers his is the only slot not working now. Paulo gets up and moves to another machine. But before he sits down it goes dark just like the other one.

"What the..." Paulo frowns in disbelief.

He looks around. And to his dismay every machine that he directly looks at around him is shutting down. The malfunction spreads rapidly and takes over the entire casino. And within seconds, every gambling machine goes dark. Paulo hears people gasping and raising their voices. Immediately following, is a PA announcement on the overhead speakers.

"Ladies and gentlemen, uh," there's a slight pause, the person talking sounds confused, "we are experiencing technical difficulties right now. Please, go to the cashier if you cannot retrieve your ticket. Thank you."

People are talking louder, some laughter, and some profanity is heard. Paulo gets up. He figures this is a good sign. He grabs the backpack and says while looking at it, "Are you doing this? You want me to leave? Is that it?"

Paulo is feeling a little anxious, and he starts to leave. He walks by several people talking passionately about their malfunctioning slots with what looks like a manager and a security guard. Paulo heads straight for the main entrance. He slows to a halt just outside the entryway to let a few people walk by. Then he hears a shout.

"Yo! Look out!" Someone yells at the top of their lungs.

Next thing Paulo realizes is a tall Native American gentleman, a casino representative, yanking him aside. What happens next is Paulo sees a blur of a large object drop next to him. Scaffolding from a remodeling project on the front of the building has collapsed, slid, and fallen right next to Paulo as he was exiting the building. Luckily, him nor anybody else was physically hurt. However, the loud impact was definitely enough to rattle everyone's nerves. Paulo is terrified. Several more representatives come over to check on him. He assures everyone he's not injured. The manager tells him to get whatever he wants from the casino delicatessen and grill, on the house. Paulo declines. Instead, he's given a $50 voucher for food. The manager had insisted.

Paulo walks back to his car. *Those slots. Each one I looked at separately shut off! What the hell was that?* He clutches the backpack tightly and starts thinking about everything that has happened since he talked to his auntie Elvie. Has every recent near-death mishap that's happened to him, including this last one, been more than just coincidence? Paulo is growing more anxious. Now he is seriously thinking of giving his auntie a call.

He drives home and goes upstairs without waking his parents. Before long, he is lying on his bed staring at his backpack. He has not taken the black velvet case out to look at the diamonds, not once. Not since he was sitting in the parking lot when he first arrived at the casino tonight. Paulo falls asleep.

CHAPTER 12
OKAY WAIT A MINUTE, BARRACUDA

ELVIE WOKE UP very early this morning. She was restless in bed all last night. In fact, she has not been sleeping very well for the past couple of nights since meeting with Paulo at the park. She has had dreams about Paulo. Bad dreams, like one where Paulo was drowning, and she was trying to rescue him. There was another where she was with her sister Mary and Alejo in a hospital waiting room. They were crying because Paulo had been in a serious car accident, and he was fighting for his life. That night Gigi had to wake her up because Elvie was crying in her sleep.

She looks at the clock on her side of the bed. It's only 4:00 AM, Wednesday. She tries to go back to sleep, but she can't stop thinking about Paulo. Elvie is worried that something might actually happen to him if he continues to keep the Almasi Ya Kifo diamonds. *I better give him a call first thing today. He needs to know that a curse is put upon someone with bad intentions possessing those diamonds,* she thought in quiet.

She lies there, hoping she will fall asleep even for a short while. Next thing she knows it's time for her morning devotional prayers. She slowly turns to sit on the side of the bed to begin reciting her morning prayers. Gigi wakes up and quietly makes her way to the kitchen to make coffee and prepare their breakfast.

· · · • • ● • • · ·

IT's 7:10 AM and Paulo is lying awake in bed. He is staring at the ceiling in deep thought. He's thinking of all the things that had happened to him these past couple of days. *It's like, I keep missing death, or death keeps missing me, or something. What's going on? Maybe it's all a coincidence or, maybe warnings? Are these diamonds really cursed? I better call Elvie today and tell her all of this.* Paulo yawns and gets up from bed. He looks at his backpack next to his pillow. But this time he doesn't bother to open it up just so he can gaze upon his sparkly treasure. He is a little apprehensive about doing that.

He is about to go downstairs when suddenly his phone starts ringing. He says to himself "Who is calling me this early? Better not be the same guy that's pranking me." Paulo is surprised to see the ID on the screen of his phone. "Auntie Elvie." He eagerly greets her.

"Good morning anak (*son*), I hope I didn't wake you up." Elvie greets in return.

"Good morning. No, I'm already up. I've been awake for a while. I was just lying here in bed thinking about all the things that have happened to me these past couple days, auntie. It's been crazy! And I really want to talk to you after work today." Paulo replies frankly.

"Look, I have to be straight with you. Please listen to me. I'm calling because I have had dreams about you fighting for your life. I'm scared because I don't want anything to happen to you, especially as you have those diamonds. I noticed your greed is consuming you. You are becoming selfish, arrogant, demanding and rude. Paulo, these are not good behaviors from a man that we raised well. These are bad. They will get you into trouble someday if you continue feeding yourself with negative energy." Elvie speaks firmly.

Paulo listens attentively to his auntie. "I'm sorry, auntie. I guess you are right. These past couple of days have been very crazy. At first, I didn't think of it as death missing me. I thought I was being lucky, because of the diamonds. It happened on three different occasions. But last night was the last straw and I want you to please help me. I'm kind of scared of these diamonds now, so maybe I can drop them to you?" Paulo suggests insistently.

"No, I don't want them! But I can help you to get rid of them. Let's talk about the details this evening."

"Really, thank you, thank you! I know I can count on you, auntie. And I am very sorry for everything. I hope you forgive me." Paulo sincerely replies.

Elvie accepts his apology and promises to call him later about the details of their plans on how to get rid of the diamonds. She is very happy that this time her nephew listened. She's smiling now, about to end the call.

"Wait one more thing. Who is this guy you hired to prank me?" Paulo aske abruptly.

"Prank you? What guy? Paulo, I don't have time for that kind of stuff. I'm a busy woman." Elvie scoffs.

"Well, because this guy called me yesterday and he said that I have something that belongs to his friend. I know he's talking about the diamonds, so I thought it's somebody you know to scare me. So, I hung up." Paulo answers.

"Paulo, like I said, I don't have time for that kind of stuff. But..." she thought for a moment. She considered the assertions and folklore she had heard over the years, "what you're telling me makes sense to what I have heard. People seek and chase after these diamonds because of the great fortune they can bring, but it all turns to bad luck or death when greed prevails. And now somebody knows where the diamonds are and, they are watching you, Paulo." Elvie's opinion is resolute, nonetheless, she replies endearingly to Paulo.

Paulo is a little more worried on hearing that. Yet, part of him seriously wants to dismiss it. Deep down inside, he does have some reservations about relinquishing the gems. *What if I could somehow control my eagerness to win and by doing that, control the good luck, control the fortune?* However, he realizes what must be done for now. They will discuss the details of how to get rid of the mysterious diamonds.

"Well, I will be waiting for your call this evening, auntie. I have to go. Oh, and by the way can I borrow a hundred dollars?" Paulo asks frankly.

"Paulo, are you kidding me?!" Elvie snaps back.

"Or buy my ticket to go to Vegas? Please? Pretty please? A hundred dollars or a ticket or both?" Paulo laughs as he asks her, but he's serious.

He wants to save all the money he has acquired over the past couple days so he could stay comfortably and gamble in Las Vegas. And treat Karen to a nice dinner, providing things went well of course.

"Okay wait a minute, barracuda. Let's talk about all that later. I know you have to go to work, and I have to go to a meeting, too. So, bye for now and I will call you this evening."

No sooner had the call ended, Elvie made another call to a dependable contact regarding the details of a diamond transporter and a contract happening, soon. She thought maybe she could plan something involving her nephew and the cursed diamonds.

CHAPTER 13
DO YOU SEE HER?

IT'S 11:00 AM Saturday, September 29. Paulo is in the economy parking lot at Los Angeles airport. He had arrived there exactly on time. He is doing precisely as his auntie had instructed. As promised, Elvie had given Paulo the details of her plan in their phone call, and had gone over everything in detail again earlier this morning. Now it is time to put that plan into action.

Paulo had parked in a particular spot as he was told to do, and had raised the trunk of his car. His backpack is in the trunk and in it were the precious diamonds. Paulo has to leave the trunk open and remain in the car. Everything up to now was, so far so good.

Elvie had told him someone working, dressed in an airport ground service uniform, would pick up the diamonds and deliver them to him inside the airport terminal. Although Paulo fully trusts his dear auntie, right now he is feeling vulnerable. He doesn't want anyone to steal his backpack. But Elvie had assured him that wouldn't happen because he would be watched the entire time as soon as he had parked. Elvie had told him to just sit and remain calm.

Looking into his passenger sideview mirror, Paulo sees an African American woman wearing an airport ramp agent uniform and yellow safety vest approach his open trunk. She had walked in-between parked cars from behind. He sees the woman pause at the rear of his car, then walk away.

Elvie calls Paulo to confirm that the woman courier had the backpack and the diamonds. He was then told to come into the terminal and proceed to the gate where the transporter would be.

When Paulo got out to close his trunk, he sees his backpack is indeed, gone. He felt a little sad. Paulo hadn't looked at the gems at all since last Tuesday night. He was too scared, yet he wants to have them back right now. It was a weird feeling that he couldn't explain. Fact is, he still covets the diamonds. He just doesn't want to honestly recognize and admit it to himself.

· · · ● ● ● ● · · ·

As Paulo passes through airport security to go to the gate, he notices Elvie and Gigi standing near the wall by the United Airlines departure gate for Florence, Italy. There are many other travelers sitting and walking by. The terminal is bustling with vacationers and the like. It is just another busy day at LAX. He swiftly walks to where the ladies are, and notices a backpack next to Elvie's wheelchair.

"Is that mine?" Paulo asks.

"Shhh... be quiet and don't touch it." Elvie shushes him.

Just then, Paulo notices the same African American woman from the parking lot walking towards them. She had entered the terminal from the ramp stairway, just outside the gate. She quickly approaches them, then stops suddenly right next to the wheelchair and the backpack. The woman is quiet. She smoothly removes Paulo's backpack from her shoulder and puts it down behind the identical looking backpack, next to the wheelchair. She kneels down and ties her left work boot shoelace, and quietly picks up the other identical backpack and walks away, rapidly disappearing into the crowd of travelers walking about.

"Pick it up now and take the jewelry box out." Elvie directs Paulo, pointing at the backpack with her cane.

"Oh, so this is my backpack?" Paulo asks happily.

"Shhh! Of course, it is! We had to get it past security. I have several people that help me get expensive valuables in and out of the country secretly. This is part of my business." Elvie says as discreetly as she can.

"So, what kind of stuff do you do?" Paulo questions.

"Really, Paulo? Do you really have to ask me that now? But you know what, it's not your business. Let's keep on track. Focus!" Elvie insists.

"Illegal stuff? Oh, I get it. This is why my dad is mad at you?" Paulo says in a joking manner.

"Paulo you better stop talking about your dad. It is really not your business, and I am serious!" Elvie is looking straight into her nephew's eyes now. Then she nods in the direction where an attractive young blonde woman is sitting. The lady is reading the August issue of Cosmopolitan magazine.

"Do you see her? Do you see that white leather tote?" Elvie asks Paulo, gesturing towards it with her eyes.

"Yes." Paulo acknowledges and sees the bag.

"Okay, now should be the time. Watch quietly."

Just then, another well-dressed older woman approaches the blonde woman sitting with the white leather tote bag. The older woman has a confident athletic build. She has medium length auburn blonde hair, stylishly cut into a bob. She is holding a bag exactly identical to the blonde woman. The older woman sits. She places her bag down, right next to the young lady's tote. Then, just as Paulo had experienced, there is an exchange. The older woman takes the other white tote bag and gets up from her seat and leaves. Now the young blonde lady sitting there has the other identical white bag that the older woman just left there.

"Whoa!" Paulo exclaims.

"Shhh! Keep your voice down." Elvie whispers heavily. She looks at him gesturing with her cane and discreetly says, "Now go over there and put the jewelry box in. Gigi will get her attention at the same time. Go!"

Gigi and Paulo split up as they walk towards the seating area. Paulo was walking quickly, keeping his eyes on Gigi so he could get the timing right, as they had planned over the phone. He almost stepped on someone's foot trying to keep up with Gigi.

"Hey, watch it, man!" A hippy looking woman says, frowning at him as she walks away.

"Oh, sorry." Paulo quickly says without looking at her. His attention is fixed on Gigi walking. Gigi turns her head to look at him. And for some curious reason, she looks surprised.

Next thing Paulo felt was him making solid contact with someone. The sound and the view of the impact brought a few gasps from some people around them. Paulo almost losses his balance as he looks forward and sees the young blonde lady falling to the floor. Her purse and cell phone and other belongings are strewn about. *Oh no... shit.* Paulo can't believe it. He has just literally run smack into the attractive blonde transporter.

"Told you to watch out, ya dumb ass!" The hippy woman could be heard in the background.

Paulo looks at Gigi, feeling helpless and at a loss for what to do next. Gigi scowls silently at him from the other row of seats. Her eyes say it all. *Really, Paulo?!* And then she points to the transporter's white tote while trying to be discreet about it at the same time.

Paulo sprang into action. He looks at the transporter who is still on the floor. She looks stunned, absolutely dumbfounded, but uninjured. Paulo notices the tote near her. He grabs it and quickly places his black velvet box inside the white tote, unobserved.

"I'm so sorry miss!" Paulo gently takes hold of the transporter's

hand. "It was an accident. I wasn't paying attention. It's all my fault."
As Paulo helps her get up, he hands her the white tote bag.

She immediately looks inside. Seeing the jewelry box, the transporter is content. What she hasn't realized is that she now has an extra case of diamonds.

"It's okay." She says, a little stunned, still. "I'm fine."

Paulo is busy picking up her things for her. He hands her a cell phone and a few other things that had fallen on the floor. He hands her the magazine, last. Then he smiles at her apologetically.

"Are you okay?" The transporter smiles back.

"Oh, yes. I am." Paulo nods. Paulo couldn't help but notice how beautiful the young lady was. She looked familiar, like a fashion model he'd seen on TV before or something.

"Well, I'm okay." She says, raising her chin confidently and putting a hand on her hip. "I'm a blackbelt, and I know how to fall." She nods and gently takes hold of his arm. "You sure you're okay my dear?"

Paulo nods like a little kid. She was really beautiful up close. And she spoke nice to him. He liked that. The kind transporter smiled and patted him on the arm.

"Good." She gives him a quaint nod, lowering her eyebrows just a slight sexy bit for a fleeting moment, as if she were posing confidently for the camera. Then, turning swiftly, she heads towards the restroom. Paulo is motionless as he watches her glide away, her hips gently swaying. His jaw has slightly lowered. *Wow.*

"Hey." Gigi is poking him from the side.

"Oh!" Paulo says, jumping a little. He puts his arm around her, relieved he has completed their intricate plan. "Yes auntie. It's done now." He looks over to Elvie. She has her head buried in the palm of her hand. Peeking at him warily between her fingers.

"Sos, Marya, Hosep (*Jesus, Mary, Joseph*), Paulo!" Elvie thumps her cane on the floor and says, "You'll give me a heart attack!"

Elvie, Gigi and Paulo are together now. They wait quietly for the attractive blonde transporter to return. Next, the boarding announcement is heard on the overhead speakers. "We are now boarding United flight twenty-six-oh-one at gate eleven for Florence. Please have your passports ready to show to the gate agent. Thank you."

They notice the transporter as she makes her way with her belongings to the boarding area. As the first-class passengers are invited to board, she quietly walks and presents her passport in turn. Next, they watch her smile and talk briefly with the gate agents. Then she walks into the jetway.

Before long, all passengers have boarded the flight. The door to the jetway closes. Then the beautiful gray and blue Boeing 747 jumbo jet pushes off the gate on time. Paulo makes his way to the windows to watch the large aircraft taxi and then takeoff.

Then he turns his attention to Elvie and Gigi who have also come to the window to watch the jumbo jet takeoff. "Hey, we did it!" Paulo cheers pointing at Elvie and Gigi. They are all smiling, laughing in relief. "So, where're you both going? Kauai to eat some of lola's (*grandmother's*) famous dinengdeng (*vegetable dish*) and tulya (*clams*)?"

"Oh yeah!" Elvie replies with a big smile, anticipating their trip to Hawaii and her delightful meal to come.

"Okay Paulo, have fun in Vegas and don't come home bankrupt." Elvie encourages him as she leans forward in her wheelchair. She gives her dear nephew a hug, and puts $200 in his palm.

"Whoa, really auntie?" Paulo is surprised. "Thank you so much. You are really the best! You do so much for me." Paulo bows his head sincerely, his palms softly clasped together. "Please hug and kiss everyone for me, especially lola (*grandmother*)."

"You're welcome. Take care of yourself and, yes, I will give everyone your regards." Elvie replies, as Gigi begins to turn her wheelchair. They wave as they quietly leave the gate area. Paulo waves back.

· · · · ● ● ● · · ·

PAULO REACHES INTO his backpack and feels around. Then, he retrieves his Southwest Airlines boarding pass for Las Vegas that his dear auntie has also purchased for him. He looks at the departure gate information. Then raises his head, smiling as he looks for the airport terminal signage to lead him to the boarding area. Paulo is really looking forward to meeting up with Karen and her friends now.

ACKNOWLEDGMENTS

To our publishing consultant and editor, Barbara Lynn. Thank you for all your support during this creative process. You have once again made this a delightful experience. Our world is a better place because of you!

To our technical advisor and friend Lester Bailey. Chief! Your remarkable experiences and stories helped us to express our characters and situations brilliantly. Thank you for your input.

And a shout-out to the Journey Book Club. Thank you for your support. You're the best!

Walk with the wise and become wise, for a companion of fools suffers harm.

-Proverbs 13:20

COMING SOON

BOOK 2 OF THE FATE DIAMOND SERIES

XENTASTIC

She's in possession of stolen diamonds, but she doesn't know.
Now someone wants them back.

Xenyatta Davenport, (Xen to those that know her) is a well-known fashion model and has graced the covers of many magazines. She's gorgeous, smart and kind, and just a little bit quirky. What isn't known, is that Xen also has a covert and ultra-confidential side profession; transporting precious gems for insurance companies.

Xen has arrived into Italy to complete her latest secret assignment. As in previous missions, there was a clandestine handover of the gems to Xen at Los Angeles International airport. Now she is patiently waiting for her Italian contact, ready to conclude the secretive delivery.

Xen's Italian contact becomes fearfully alarmed to recognize the cursed Almasi Ya Kifo diamonds are part of the delivery. She is beyond disturbed and vehemently refuses to accept the diamonds and thrusts them back to Xen.

Xen had unknowingly received the mysterious Almasi Ya Kifo diamonds as part of her assignment. Now Xen is wondering how she ended up with them?

Like others before her, Xen will experience some of the strange unquantifiable energy that the diamonds retain. What will those effects be... enchanting or precarious?

ALSO BY MAURY K. DOWNS

Aliens make a stealth landing late at night. They possess a unique capability never seen before. The mission becomes compromised when Brian discovers their presence. The aliens confront him, but he's unharmed. The aliens decide to continue with the mission and solicit Brian's help. Will they complete their important mission? Only destiny knows.

www.ingramcontent.com/pod-product-compliance
Lightning Source LLC
Chambersburg PA
CBHW070412200726
48294CB00003B/1175